MRS. KORNER SINS HER MERCIES

By

Jerome K. Jerome

British Library Cataloguing-in-Publication Data
A catalogue record for this book is available from the
British Library

Jerome K. Jerome

Jerome Klapka Jerome was born in Walsall, England in 1859. Both his parents died while he was in his early teens, and he was forced to quit school to support himself. Jerome worked for a number of years collecting coal along railway tracks, before trying his hand at acting, journalism, teaching and soliciting. At long last, in 1885, he had some success with *On the Stage – and Off,* a comic memoir of his experiences with an acting troupe. Jerome produced a number of essays over the following years, and married in 1888, spending the honeymoon in "a little boat" on the Thames.

In 1889, Jerome published his most successful and best-remembered work, *Three Men in a Boat.* Featuring himself and two of his friends encountering humorous situations while floating down the Thames in a small boat, the book was an instant success, and has never been out of print. In fact, its popularity was such that the number of registered Thames boats went up fifty percent in the year following its publication. With the financial security provided by *Three Men in a Boat,* Jerome was able to dedicate himself fully to writing, producing eleven more novels and a number of anthologies of short fiction.

In 1926, Jerome published his autobiography, *My Life and Times.* He died a year later, aged 68.

"I do mean it," declared Mrs. Korner, "I like a man to be a man."

"But you would not like Christopher—I mean Mr. Korner—to be that sort of man," suggested her bosom friend.

"I don't mean that I should like it if he did it often. But I should like to feel that he was able to be that sort of man.—Have you told your master that breakfast is ready?" demanded Mrs. Korner of the domestic staff, entering at the moment with three boiled eggs and a teapot.

"Yus, I've told 'im," replied the staff indignantly.

The domestic staff at Acacia Villa, Ravenscourt Park, lived in a state of indignation. It could be heard of mornings and evenings saying its prayers indignantly.

"What did he say?"

"Said 'e'11 be down the moment 'e's dressed."

"Nobody wants him to come before," commented Mrs. Korner. "Answered me that he was putting on his collar when I called up to him five minutes ago."

"Answer yer the same thing now, if yer called up to 'im agen, I 'spect," was the opinion of the staff. "Was on 'is 'ands and knees when I looked in, scooping round under the bed for 'is collar stud."

Mrs. Korner paused with the teapot in her hand. "Was he talking?"

"Talkin'? Nobody there to talk to; I 'adn't got no time to stop and chatter."

"I mean to himself," explained Mrs. Korner. "He—he wasn't swearing?" There was a note of eagerness, almost of hope, in Mrs. Korner's voice.

"Swearin'! 'E! Why, 'e don't know any."

"Thank you," said Mrs. Korner. "That will do, Harriet; you may go."

Mrs Korner put down the teapot with a bang. "The very girl," said Mrs. Korner bitterly, "the very girl despises him."

"Perhaps," suggested Miss Greene, "he had been swearing and had finished."

But Mrs. Korner was not to be comforted. "Finished! Any other man would have been swearing all the time."

"Perhaps," suggested the kindly bosom friend, ever the one to plead the cause of the transgressor, "perhaps he was swearing, and she did not hear him. You see, if he had his head well underneath the bed—"

The door opened.

"Sorry I am late," said Mr. Korner, bursting cheerfully into the room. It was a point with Mr. Korner always to be cheerful in the morning. "Greet the day with a smile and it will leave you with a blessing," was the motto Mrs. Korner, this day a married woman of six months and three weeks standing had heard her husband murmur before getting out of bed on precisely two hundred and two occasions. The Motto entered largely into the scheme of Mr. Korner's life. Written in fine copperplate upon cards all of the same size, a choice selection counselled him each morning from the rim of his shaving-glass.

"Did you find it?" asked Mrs. Korner.

"It is most extraordinary," replied Mr. Korner, as he seated himself at the breakfast-table. "I saw it go under the bed with my own eyes. Perhaps—"

"Don't ask me to look for it," interrupted Mrs. Korner. "Crawling about on their hands and knees, knocking their heads against iron bedsteads, would be enough to make some people swear." The emphasis was on the "some."

"It is not bad training for the character," hinted Mr. Korner, "occasionally to force oneself to perform patiently tasks calculated—"

"If you get tied up in one of those long sentences of yours, you will never get out in time to eat your breakfast," was the fear of Mrs. Korner.

"I should be sorry for anything to happen to it," remarked Mr. Korner, "its intrinsic value may perhaps—"

"I will look for it after breakfast," volunteered the amiable Miss Greene. "I am good at finding things."

"I can well believe it," the gallant Mr. Korner assured her, as with the handle of his spoon he peeled his egg. "From such bright eyes as yours, few—"

"You've only got ten minutes," his wife reminded him. "Do get on with your breakfast."

"I should like," said Mr. Korner, "to finish a speech occasionally."

"You never would," asserted Mrs. Korner.

"I should like to try," sighed Mr. Korner, "one of these days—"

"How did you sleep, dear? I forgot to ask you," questioned Mrs. Korner of the bosom friend.

"I am always restless in a strange bed the first night," explained Miss Greene. "I daresay, too, I was a little excited."

"I could have wished," said Mr. Korner, "it had been a better example of the delightful art of the dramatist. When one goes but seldom to the theatre—"

"One wants to enjoy oneself" interrupted Mrs. Korner.

"I really do not think," said the bosom friend, "that I have ever laughed so much in all my life."

"It was amusing. I laughed myself," admitted Mr. Korner. "At the same time I cannot help thinking that to treat drunkenness as a theme—"

"He wasn't drunk," argued Mrs. Korner, "he was just jovial."

"My dear!" Mr. Korner Corrected her, "he simply couldn't stand."

"He was much more amusing than some people who can," retorted Mrs. Korner.

"It is possible, my dear Aimee," her husband pointed out to her, "for a man to be amusing without being drunk; also for a man to be drunk without—"

"Oh, a man is all the better," declared Mrs. Korner, "for letting himself go occasionally."

"My dear—"

"You, Christopher, would be all the better for letting yourself go—occasionally."

"I wish," said Mr. Korner, as he passed his empty cup, "you would not say things you do not mean. Anyone hearing you—"

"If there's one thing makes me more angry than another," said Mrs. Korner, "it is being told I say things that I do not mean."

"Why say them then?" suggested Mr. Korner.

"I don't. I do—I mean I do mean them," explained Mrs. Korner.

"You can hardly mean, my dear," persisted her husband, "that you really think I should be all the better for getting drunk—even occasionally."

"I didn't say drunk; I said 'going it.'"

"But I do 'go it' in moderation," pleaded Mr. Korner, "'Moderation in all things,' that is my motto."

"I know it," returned Mrs. Korner.

"A little of everything and nothing—" this time Mr. Korner interrupted himself. "I fear," said Mr. Korner, rising, "we must postpone the further discussion of this interesting topic. If you would not mind stepping out with me into the passage, dear, there are one or two little matters connected with the house—"

Host and hostess squeezed past the visitor and closed the door behind them. The visitor continued eating.

"I do mean it," repeated Mrs. Korner, for the third time, reseating herself a minute later at the table. "I would give anything—anything," reiterated the lady recklessly, "to see Christopher more like the ordinary sort of man."

"But he has always been the sort—the sort of man he is," her bosom friend reminded her.

"Oh, during the engagement, of course, one expects a man to be perfect. I didn't think he was going to keep it up."

"He seems to me," said Miss Greene, "a dear, good fellow. You are one of those people who never know when they are well off."

"I know he is a good fellow," agreed Mrs. Korner, "and I am very fond of him. It is just because I am fond of him that I hate feeling ashamed of him. I want him to be a manly man, to do the things that other men do."

"Do all the ordinary sort of men swear and get occasionally drunk?"

"Of course they do," asserted Mrs. Korner, in a tone of authority. "One does not want a man to be a milksop."

"Have you ever seen a drunken man?" inquired the bosom friend, who was nibbling sugar.

"Heaps," replied Mrs. Korner, who was sucking marmalade off her fingers.

By which Mrs. Korner meant that some half a dozen times in her life she had visited the play, choosing by preference the lighter form of British drama. The first time she witnessed the real thing, which happened just precisely a month later, long after the conversation here recorded had been forgotten by the parties most concerned, no one could have been more utterly astonished than was Mrs. Korner.

How it came about Mr. Korner was never able to fully satisfy himself. Mr. Korner was not the type that serves the purpose of the temperance lecturer. His "first glass" he had drunk more years ago than he could recollect, and since had tasted the varied contents of many others. But never before had Mr. Korner exceeded, nor been tempted to exceed, the limits of his favourite virtue, moderation.

"We had one bottle of claret between us," Mr. Korner would often recall to his mind, "of which he drank the greater part. And then he brought out the little green flask. He said it was made from pears—that in Peru they kept it specially for Children's parties. Of course, that may have been his joke; but in any case I cannot see how just one glass—I wonder could I have taken more than one glass while he was talking." It was a point that worried Mr. Korner.

The "he" who had talked, possibly, to such bad effect was a distant cousin of Mr. Korner's, one Bill Damon, chief mate of the steamship *La Fortuna*. Until their chance meeting that afternoon in Leadenhall Street, they had not seen each other since they were boys together. The *Fortuna* was leaving St. Katherine's Docks early the next morning bound for South America, and it might be years before they met again. As Mr. Damon pointed out, Fate, by thus throwing them into each other's arms, clearly intended they should have a cosy dinner together that very evening in the captain's cabin of the *Fortuna*.

Mr. Korner, returning to the office, despatched to Ravenscourt Park an express letter, announcing the strange news that he might not be home that evening much before ten, and at half-past six, for the first time since his marriage, directed his steps away from home and Mrs. Korner.

The two friends talked of many things. And later on they spoke of sweethearts and of wives. Mate Damon's experiences had apparently been wide and varied. They talked—or, rather, the mate talked, and Mr. Korner listened—of the olive-tinted beauties of the Spanish Main, of the dark-eyed passionate creoles, of the blond Junos of the Californian valleys. The mate had theories concerning the care and management of women: theories that, if the mate's word could be relied upon, had stood the test of studied application. A new world opened out to Mr. Korner; a world where lovely women worshipped with doglike devotion men who, though loving them in return, knew how to be their masters. Mr. Korner, warmed gradually from cold disapproval to bubbling appreciation, sat entranced. Time alone set a limit to the recital of the mate's adventures. At eleven o'clock the cook reminded them that the captain and the pilot might be aboard at any moment. Mr. Korner, surprised at the lateness of the hour, took a long and tender farewell of his cousin, and found St. Katherine's Docks one of the most bewildering places out of which he had ever tried to escape. Under a lamp-post in the Minories, it suddenly occurred to Mr. Korner that he was an unappreciated man. Mrs. Korner never said and did the sort of things by means of which the beauties of the Southern Main endeavoured feebly to express their consuming passion for gentlemen superior in no way—as far as he could see—to Mr. Korner himself. Thinking over the sort of things Mrs. Korner did say and did do, tears sprung into Mr. Korner's eyes. Noticing that a policeman was eyeing him with curiosity, he dashed them aside and hurried on. Pacing the platform of the Mansion House Station, where it is always draughty, the thought of his wrongs returned to him with renewed force. Why was there no trace of doglike devotion about Mrs. Korner? The fault—so he bitterly told himself—the fault was his. "A woman loves her master; it is her instinct," mused Mr. Korner to himself. "Damme," thought Mr. Korner, "I don't believe that half her time she knows I am her master."

"Go away," said Mr. Korner to a youth of pasty appearance who, with open mouth, had stopped immediately in front of him.

"I'm fond o' listening," explained the pasty youth.

"Who's talking?" demanded Mr. Korner.

"You are," replied the pasty youth.

It is a long journey from the city to Ravenscourt Park, but the task of planning out the future life of Mrs. Korner and himself kept Mr. Korner wide awake and interested. When he got out of the train the thing chiefly troubling him was the three-quarters of a mile of muddy road stretching between him and his determination to make things clear to Mrs. Korner then and there.

The sight of Acacia Villa, suggesting that everybody was in bed and asleep, served to further irritate him. A dog-like wife would have been sitting up to see if there was anything he wanted. Mr. Korner, acting on the advice of his own brass plate, not only knocked but also rang. As the door did not immediately fly open, he continued to knock and ring. The window of the best bedroom on the first floor opened.

"Is that you?" said the voice of Mrs. Korner. There was, as it happened, a distinct suggestion of passion in Mrs. Korner's voice, but not of the passion Mr. Korner was wishful to inspire. It made him a little more angry than he was before.

"Don't you talk to me with your head out of the window as if this were a gallanty show. You come down and open the door," commanded Mr. Korner.

"Haven't you got your latchkey?" demanded Mrs. Korner.

For answer Mr. Korner attacked the door again. The window closed. The next moment but six or seven, the door was opened with such suddenness that Mr. Korner, still gripping the knocker, was borne inward in a flying attitude. Mrs. Korner had descended the stairs ready with a few remarks. She had not anticipated that Mr. Korner, usually slow of speech, could be even readier.

"Where's my supper?" indignantly demanded Mr. Korner, still supported by the knocker.

Mrs. Korner, too astonished for words, simply stared.

"Where's my supper?" repeated Mr. Korner, by this time worked up into genuine astonishment that it was not ready for him. "What's everybody mean, going off to bed, when the masterororous hasn't had his supper?"

"Is anything the matter, dear?" was heard the voice of Miss Greene, speaking from the neighbourhood of the first landing.

"Come in, Christopher," pleaded Mrs. Korner, "please come in, and let me shut the door."

Mrs. Korner was the type of young lady fond of domineering with a not un-graceful hauteur over those accustomed to yield readily to her; it is a type that is easily frightened.

"I wan' grilled kinneys-on-toast," explained Mr. Korner, exchanging the knocker for the hat-stand, and wishing the next moment that he had not. "Don' let's 'avareytalk about it. Unnerstan'? I dowan' any talk about it."

"What on earth am I to do?" whispered the terrified Mrs. Korner to her bosom friend, "there isn't a kidney in the house."

"I should poach him a couple of eggs," suggested the helpful bosom friend; "put plenty of Cayenne pepper on them. Very likely he won't remember."

Mr. Korner allowed himself to be persuaded into the dining-room, which was also the breakfast parlour and the library. The two ladies, joined by the hastily clad staff, whose chronic indignation seemed to have vanished in face of the first excuse for it that Acacia Villa had afforded her, made haste to light the kitchen fire.

"I should never have believed it," whispered the white-faced Mrs. Korner, "never."

"Makes yer know there's a man about the 'ouse, don't it?" chirped the delighted staff. Mrs. Korner, for answer, boxed the girl's ears; it relieved her feelings to a slight extent.

The staff retained its equanimity, but the operations of Mrs. Korner and her bosom friend were retarded rather than assisted by the voice of Mr. Korner, heard every quarter of a minute, roaring out fresh directions.

"I dare not go in alone," said Mrs. Korner, when all things were in order on the tray. So the bosom friend followed her, and the staff brought up the rear.

"What's this?" frowned Mr. Korner. "I told you chops."

"I'm so sorry, dear," faltered Mrs. Korner, "but there weren't any in the house."

"In a perfectly organizedouse, such as for the future I meanterave," continued Mr. Korner, helping himself to beer, "there should always be chopanteak. Unnerstanme? chopanteak!"

"I'll try and remember, dear," said Mrs. Korner.

"Pearsterme," said Mr. Korner, between mouthfuls, "you're norrer sort of housekeeper I want."

"I'll try to be, dear," pleaded Mrs. Korner.

"Where's your books?" Mr. Korner suddenly demanded.

"My books?" repeated Mrs. Korner, in astonishment.

Mr. Korner struck the corner of the table with his fist, which made most things in the room, including Mrs. Korner, jump.

"Don't you defy me, my girl," said Mr. Korner. "You know whatermean, your housekeepin' books."

They happened to be in the drawer of the chiffonier. Mrs. Korner produced them, and passed them to her husband with a trembling hand. Mr. Korner, opening one by hazard, bent over it with knitted brows.

"Pearsterme, my girl, you can't add," said Mr. Korner.

"I—I was always considered rather good at arithmetic, as a girl," stammered Mrs. Korner.

"What you mayabeen as a girl, and what—twenner-seven and nine?" fiercely questioned Mr. Korner.

"Thirty-eight—seven," commenced to blunder the terrified Mrs. Korner.

"Know your nine tables or don't you?" thundered Mr. Korner.

"I used to," sobbed Mrs. Korner.

"Say it," commanded Mr. Korner.

"Nine times one are nine," sobbed the poor little woman, "nine times two—"

"Goron," said Mr. Korner sternly.

She went on steadily, in a low monotone, broken by stifled sobs. The dreary rhythm of the repetition may possibly have assisted. As she mentioned fearfully that nine times eleven were ninety-nine, Miss Greene pointed stealthily toward the table. Mrs. Korner, glancing up fearfully, saw that the eyes of her lord and master were closed; heard the rising snore that issued from his head, resting between the empty beer-jug and the cruet stand.

"He will be all right," counselled Miss Greene. "You go to bed and lock yourself in. Harriet and I will see to his breakfast in the morning. It will be just as well for you to be out of the way."

And Mrs. Korner, only too thankful for some one to tell her what to do, obeyed in all things.

Toward seven o'clock the sunlight streaming into the room caused Mr. Korner first to blink, then yawn, then open half an eye.

"Greet the day with a smile," murmured Mr. Korner, sleepily, "and it will—"

Mr. Korner sat up suddenly and looked about him. This was not bed. The fragments of a jug and glass lay scattered round his feet. To the tablecloth an overturned cruet-stand mingled with egg gave colour. A tingling sensation about his head called for investigation. Mr. Korner was forced to the conclusion that somebody had been trying to make a salad of him—somebody with an exceptionally heavy hand for mustard. A sound directed Mr. Korner's attention to the door.

The face of Miss Greene, portentously grave, was peeping through the jar.

Mr. Korner rose. Miss Greene entered stealthily, and, closing the door, stood with her back against it.

"I suppose you know what—what you've done?" suggested Miss Greene.

She spoke in a sepulchral tone; it chilled poor Mr. Korner to the bone.

"It is beginning to come back to me, but not—not very clearly," admitted Mr. Korner.

"You came home drunk—very drunk," Miss Greene informed him, "at two o'clock in the morning. The noise you made must have awakened half the street."

A groan escaped from his parched lips.

"You insisted upon Aimee cooking you a hot supper."

"I insisted!" Mr. Korner glanced down upon the table. "And—and she did it!"

"You were very violent," explained Miss Greene; "we were terrified at you, all three of us." Regarding the pathetic object in front of her, Miss Greene found it difficult to recollect that a few hours before she really had been frightened of it. Sense of duty alone restrained her present inclination to laugh.

"While you sat there, eating your supper," continued Miss Greene remorselessly, "you made her bring you her books."

Mr. Korner had passed the stage when anything could astonish him.

"You lectured her about her housekeeping." There was a twinkle in the eye of Mrs. Korner's bosom friend. But lightning could have flashed before Mr. Korner's eyes without his noticing it just then.

"You told her that she could not add, and you made her say her tables."

"I made her—" Mr. Korner spoke in the emotionless tones of one merely desiring information. "I made Aimee say her tables?"

"Her nine times," nodded Miss Greene.

Mr. Korner sat down upon his chair and stared with stony eyes into the future.

"What's to be done?" said Mr. Korner, "she'll never forgive me; I know her. You are not chaffing me?" he cried with a momentary gleam of hope. "I really did it?"

"You sat in that very chair where you are sitting now and ate poached eggs, while she stood opposite to you and said her nine times table. At the end of it, seeing you had gone to sleep yourself, I persuaded her to go to bed. It was three o'clock, and we thought you would not mind." Miss Greene drew up a chair, and, with her elbows on the table, looked across at Mr. Korner. Decidedly there was a twinkle in the eyes of Mrs. Korner's bosom friend.

"You'll never do it again," suggested Miss Greene.

"Do you think it possible," cried Mr. Korner, "that she may forgive me?"

"No, I don't," replied Miss Greene. At which Mr. Korner's face fell back to zero. "I think the best way out will be for you to forgive her."

The idea did not even amuse him. Miss Greene glanced round to satisfy herself that the door was still closed, and listened a moment to assure herself of the silence.

"Don't you remember," Miss Greene took the extra precaution to whisper it, "the talk we had at breakfast-time the first morning of my visit, when Aimee said you would be all the better for 'going it' occasionally?"

Yes, slowly it came back to Mr. Korner. But she only said "going it," Mr. Korner recollected to his dismay.

"Well, you've been 'going it,'" persisted Miss Greene. "Besides, she did not mean 'going it.' She meant the real thing, only she did not like to say the word. We talked about it after you had gone. She said she would give anything to see you more like the ordinary man. And that is her idea of the ordinary man."

Mr. Korner's sluggishness of comprehension irritated Miss Greene. She leaned across the table and shook him. "Don't you understand? You have done it on purpose to teach her a lesson. It is she who has got to ask you to forgive her."

"You think—?"

"I think, if you manage it properly, it will be the best day's work you have ever done. Get out of the house before she wakes. I shall say nothing to her. Indeed, I shall not have the time; I must catch the ten o'clock from Paddington. When you come home this evening, you talk first; that's what you've got to do." And Mr. Korner, in his excitement, kissed the bosom friend before he knew what he had done.

Mrs. Korner sat waiting for her husband that evening in the drawing-room. She was dressed as for a journey, and about the corners of her mouth were lines familiar to Christopher, the sight of which sent his heart into his boots. Fortunately, he recovered himself in time to greet her with a smile. It was not the smile he had been rehearsing half the day, but that it was a smile of any sort astonished the words away from Mrs. Korner's lips, and gave him the inestimable advantage of first speech.

"Well," said Mr. Korner cheerily, "and how did you like it?"

For the moment Mrs. Korner feared her husband's new complaint had already reached the chronic stage, but his still smiling face reassured her—to that extent at all events.

"When would you like me to 'go it' again? Oh, come," continued Mr. Korner in response to his wife's bewilderment, "you surely have not forgotten the talk we had at breakfast-time—the first morning of Mildred's visit. You hinted how much more attractive I should be for occasionally 'letting myself go!'"

Mr. Korner, watching intently, perceived that upon Mrs. Korner recollection was slowly forcing itself.

"I was unable to oblige you before," explained Mr. Korner, "having to keep my head clear for business, and not knowing what the effect upon one might be. Yesterday I did my best, and I hope you are pleased with me. Though, if you could see your way to being content—just for the present and until I get more used to it—with a similar performance not oftener than once a fortnight, say, I should be grateful," added Mr. Korner.

"You mean—" said Mrs. Korner, rising.

"I mean, my dear," said Mr. Korner, "that almost from the day of our marriage you have made it clear that you regard me as a milksop. You have got your notion of men from silly books and sillier plays, and your trouble is that I am not like them. Well, I've shown you that, if you insist upon it, I can be like them."

"But you weren't," argued Mrs. Korner, "not a bit like them."

"I did my best," repeated Mr. Korner; "we are not all made alike. That was *my* drunk."

"I didn't say 'drunk.'"

"But you meant it," interrupted Mr. Korner. "We were talking about drunken men. The man in the play was drunk. You thought him amusing."

"He was amusing," persisted Mrs. Korner, now in tears. "I meant that sort of drunk."

"His wife," Mr. Korner reminded her, "didn't find him amusing. In the third act she was threatening to return home to her mother, which, if I may judge from finding you here with all your clothes on, is also the idea that has occurred to you."

"But you—you were so awful," whimpered Mrs. Korner.

"What did I do?" questioned Mr. Korner.

"You came hammering at the door—"

"Yes, yes, I remember that. I wanted my supper, and you poached me a couple of eggs. What happened after that?"

The recollection of that crowning indignity lent to her voice the true note of tragedy.

"You made me say my tables—my nine times!"

Mr. Korner looked at Mrs. Korner, and Mrs. Korner looked at Mr. Korner, and for a while there was silence.

"Were you—were you really a little bit on," faltered Mrs. Korner, "or only pretending?"

"Really," confessed Mr. Korner. "For the first time in my life. If you are content, for the last time also."

"I am sorry," said Mrs. Korner, "I have been very silly. Please forgive me."

www.ingramcontent.com/pod-product-compliance
Lightning Source LLC
Chambersburg PA
CBHW030244180626
46810CB00008B/3280